1

Magnificent Mabel
and the Egg and
Spoon Race

Everyone thinks sports day is
fun.

Sports day is not fun.

Sports day is unfair.

At sports day I am always
being partnered with people who
get cross if I come last – even
if it's by an accident and NOT
MY FAULT.

Last year, I had to be on a
team with Edward Silitoe and

Magnificent
MABEL

...nd the Egg and Spoon Race

...uth
...quayle

...lia
...istians

First published in the UK in 2021 by Nosy Crow Ltd
The Crow's Nest, 14 Baden Place,
Crosby Row, London SE1 1YW

Nosy Crow and associated logos are trademarks and/or registered
trademarks of Nosy Crow Ltd

Text © Ruth Quayle, 2021
Illustrations © Julia Christians, 2021

The right of Ruth Quayle and Julia Christians to be identified as
the author and illustrator respectively of this work has been asserted by them
in accordance with the Copyright, Designs and Patents Act, 1988

1 3 5 7 9 10 8 6 4 2

A CIP catalogue record for this book is available from the British Library

Printed and bound in the UK by Clays Ltd, Elcograf S.p.A.

Papers used by Nosy Crow are made from wood grown in
sustainable forests.

ISBN: 978 1 83994 012 5

www.nosycrow.com

the problem with being on a team with someone else is that your scores get added together and if you're not a rusher you can't help letting your team down.

Last year Edward Silitoe got really cross with me. He said that if I hadn't been so slow getting in my sack at the beginning of the sack race we would have won.

But the reason I was slow
was because I spotted some rare
moths at the bottom of my sack
and I had a feeling that those
moths were making a nest for
their eggs.

So then I had to take an extra-
long time getting into that sack
because if those moths WERE
making a nest, I didn't want to

squash all those precious baby
moth eggs.

"Edward Silitoe," I explained.
"Winning races is not as
important as saving the lives of

living creatures."

But Edward Silitoe does not care about living creatures.

Edward Silitoe cares about being fast.

That is why for this year's sports day I did not want to be on a team with someone who is always in a rush like Edward Silitoe.

I wanted to be on a team with

someone fun and jolly.

When it was time for Mr Messenger to announce our teams my heart began to wobble and I felt quite jumpy.

I thought, I don't feel well.

I thought, I'd better not sit anywhere near Edward Silitoe.

That's why I pushed myself right up against Lottie Clark. Lottie Clark has trainers that light up and Lottie Clark prefers giggling to rushing. Lottie Clark is exactly my sort of person. Also, Lottie Clark has a brand new puppy.

But pushing right up against Lottie Clark did not fool Mr Messenger.

He did not even

care that I wanted to be in a team with Lottie Clark. He told me and Lottie Clark to sit up straight and stop giggling. He said I had to go and sit with Edward Silitoe and BE HIS PARTNER for the whole of sports day.

Then Mr Messenger said the first event was a running race.

Sometimes life isn't even fair.

At the start of the running race, Edward Silitoe said, "You'd better start stretching, Mabel Chase." He said, "We won't win if you don't stretch."

Edward Silitoe bent down and touched his toes.

I thought, if Edward Silitoe thinks that's stretching he's wrong.

I thought, that's not what

they do at the Olympics on television.

I thought, I'm really surprised that Edward Silitoe doesn't know about Olympic stretches.

I thought, I'll show him.

I swung my arms from side to side and each time I swung my arms they went a bit faster.

Olympic stretching was actually really fun and it was

quite jolly too.

It wasn't my fault that I accidentally hit Edward Silitoe a teeny bit hard on his arm.

"Mr Messenger!" shouted Edward Silitoe. "Mabel Chase is whacking me."

"That's not whacking, Edward Silitoe," I said. "That's

stretching."

Mr Messenger gave me and
Edward Silitoe a long look.
He said it was time to stop

stretching and get on with the race. Then he blew the whistle.

Everyone in Class One rushed off at toppity speed.

Everyone except me.

I could only run VERY VERY slowly because I hadn't been allowed to finish my stretching.

That's why I came last.

Edward Silitoe was furious.

He said, "You're not even

trying, Mabel."

He said, "Next time, I want
you to fly like the wind."

I nodded at Edward Silitoe
and said, "Flying is not a

problem for me," and this was actually the truth because if there's one thing I am mad about, it is flying.

Flying is one of my favourite things.

But I was slightly worried because how can you fly like the wind if you don't have any wings?

I was still thinking about

the best way to get some wings when Mr Messenger told us to line up for the obstacle race.

I thought, I bet everybody else has got hidden wings under their PE tops.

I thought, why didn't I get any wings?

I thought, I need to come up with a plan.

Then Mr Messenger blew the

 whistle and everyone set off in a mad rush.

In the obstacle race you have to do all sorts of things like jump over prickly hay bales and carry freezing cold water without spilling it but the first thing you have to do is rummage around in a pile of fancy-dress clothes

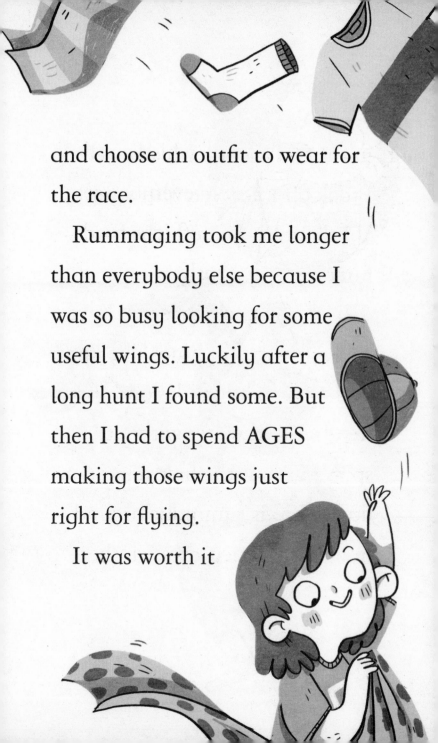

and choose an outfit to wear for the race.

Rummaging took me longer than everybody else because I was so busy looking for some useful wings. Luckily after a long hunt I found some. But then I had to spend AGES making those wings just right for flying.

It was worth it

in the end though because when
I took off I flew like the wind.

I thought, flying is the best
fun ever.

I thought, I'm definitely going to win now.

Then I looked around me.

Nobody else in Class One was flying.

Everybody else in Class One had finished the obstacle race and they were all cooling down under the oak tree with their water bottles.

Well, everybody except

Edward Silitoe, who was running
towards me and shouting rudely.

"Mabel Chase!" shouted
Edward Silitoe. "You've forgotten
to jump the hay bale and you've

missed out the water section. You are the slowest person in the whole of Class One and I wish you weren't my partner."

Then Edward Silitoe told me that our team had been disqualified.

I landed right next to Edward Silitoe and I gave him a look. I said, "Edward Silitoe, it's not my fault that wings take a long time to make."

After that I couldn't really say anything else to Edward Silitoe because my tongue sort of slipped out of my mouth and pointed in his direction.

Edward Silitoe said, "If you don't stop sticking your tongue out at me, Mabel Chase, then I'm going to tell a teacher."

Another reason why I do

not like being Edward Silitoe's partner on sports day is because he is a tell-tale and I am not keen on tell-tales. But I had to stop sticking out my tongue because it was time for the egg and spoon race.

Mrs Woodlea came over and gave everyone in our class an old silver spoon, then she went round again and gave everyone

a REAL LIFE
EGG.

She told us all to place our
eggs on our spoons and to line
up sensibly.

I thought, I'm going to show
Edward Silitoe that I am not the
slowest person in Class One.

I thought, this time I won't
come last or get disqualified.

This time I will rush.

When Mr Messenger blew the whistle I set off at toppity speed.

But then I caught sight of the speckly brown egg wobbling at the end of my spoon.

That's when I remembered that teeny tiny baby chicks live inside real-life eggs.

I thought, I am not going to let a teeny tiny baby chick get smashed to smithereens.

I thought, somebody has
to look after this teeny tiny
unhatched chick.

I stopped running and I
waited for my brown speckly
egg to stop wobbling on my
spoon. Then I held my spoon
VERY, VERY carefully and I set
off towards the finish line.

I was so worried about that

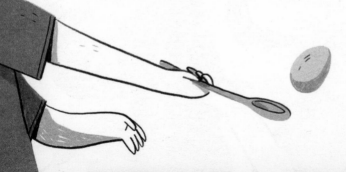

teeny tiny baby chick that I did not even dare to rush. I walked VERY, VERY slowly. And all the time I was walking I kept an eye on that brown speckly egg so it

wouldn't wobble off my spoon.

That is why it took me such a long time to get to the finish line and that is why I came last.

I thought, Edward Silitoe is going to be SO CROSS with me.

I thought, I'd better hide.

But before I could get to my secret hiding place at the back of the PE shed, Edward Silitoe ran up to me.

My heart went all sinky.

"You don't have to say anything, Edward Silitoe," I told him. "I know I'm a slow coach and I don't even care."

I waited for Edward Silitoe to start shouting but Edward Silitoe did not shout and he didn't look cross either. He looked happy.

Edward Silitoe jumped up and

down, all smiley, like he needed a wee. He said, "You've won! You've won!"

Then Mr Messenger walked up to me and he had a big smile on his face too.

Mr Messenger turned to everybody and he said, "Mabel has taught us all a very important lesson. She has shown us that going slowly can

sometimes be just as effective
as going fast." He said, "Mabel
was the only person NOT TO
RUSH and that is why she was
the only person not to drop their
egg." He said, "Three cheers for

Mabel Chase."

Everybody in Class One shouted, "Hip Hip Hooray", and Mr Messenger put a gold medal round my neck.

For a long time I did not say one word because I was so busy looking at my medal. When you win something like a gold medal you can't let it out of your sight.

I was so happy that I didn't

even get cross when Elsa
Kavinsky tried telling me
that my gold medal was

made out of plastic and not
even valuable. I said, "Actually,
Elsa Kavinsky, I can tell that
my medal is made of real gold
because it is very heavy and,
also, when I rub it with my
T-shirt it shines like treasure."

Luckily Lottie Clark did not
say that my medal was made of
plastic. Lottie Clark said, "Well
done, Mabel!" and her eyes

twinkled a bit like fairy lights.

I thought, Lottie Clark is a really nice person.

I thought, I wonder if Lottie Clark will let me try on her trainers that light up.

I thought, I'll ask her.

Lottie Clark said I could borrow her lighting-up trainers for the rest of the day if I wanted. This was so kind of

Lottie Clark that I let her wear my real gold medal for ten seconds.

After that, Lottie Clark and I spent nearly the whole afternoon giggling and flying and Lottie Clark said I could come to her house next week because SHE WANTS TO SHOW ME HER NEW PUPPY.

It was the best day of my life.

That night at bedtime, I
put my real gold medal under
my pillow and I put my hand
around it to keep it safe from
burglars and also to stop my
sister Meg from trying to steal

it in the middle of the night.

I thought, I can't wait to meet Lottie Clark's puppy next week.

I thought, Sports Day was really fun and jolly this year.

I thought, it's a good job SOMEONE on my team knew that saving the lives of living creatures is more important than rushing.

2

Magnificent Mabel
and the
Class Play

My teacher Mr Messenger is mad about acting.

In Class One we do a new play every term.

This is not too bad because acting is easier than maths and comprehension.

Also acting is fun.

But acting is not fun when SOME people get all the good parts.

That is the main problem with school plays.

Like for instance, last term Hannah Petrie was Robin Hood and Harry Cox was the Sheriff of Nottingham.

Hannah Petrie had twenty-seven lines AND a bow and arrow.

Harry Cox was allowed to carry a real silver sword.

Harry Cox and Hannah Petrie would not stop practising sword fighting.

Harry Cox and Hannah Petrie were QUITE boasty.

Last term, I did not have one single line to remember because I was a market seller and market sellers do not speak.

Market sellers stand still and hold vegetables.

Market sellers wear brown tunics.

I told my mum that being a market seller was not a pleasant

experience.

I said, "Being a market seller is a tragic situation for me."

"Don't worry, Mabel," said Mum, all chirpy. "I'm sure you'll get a good part in next term's play."

But the new play took AGES to come along because Mr Messenger made us do non-stop learning for months.

Luckily a few weeks ago, Mr Messenger told us that it was time to start rehearsing the new play.

He said the new play was going to be A SHOWSTOPPER.

I got a bit jumpety.

"Mr Messenger," I said in my most pleading

voice. "Can I be Robin Hood
this time?" Then I said, "Thank
you very much, Mr Messenger",
because Mr Messenger is keen on
good manners.

But Mr Messenger said this
term's play was not about
Robin Hood. He said it was
about a man called William
Shakespeare who was a famous
writer. Mr Messenger said

William Shakespeare died
hundreds of years ago but
everybody remembers him
because he was VERY, VERY
CLEVER.

I sat down. I was not happy.

Writers don't carry bows and
arrows and have sword fights.

Writers are not even
interesting.

But then Mr Messenger held

 up a picture of William Shakespeare. I looked closely at that picture.

William Shakespeare was not what I was expecting. He had QUITE interesting clothes. William Shakespeare had a VERY interesting beard.

I did not shout out. I put my hand up SENSIBLY and waited for Mr Messenger to spot me.

After a long time Mr Messenger turned to me and said, "Yes, Mabel?"

"Mr Messenger," I said. "Will the person playing William Shakespeare wear an interesting beard?"

Mr Messenger smiled and

picked up a bag on his desk.

"As a matter of fact," he said, "I have William Shakespeare's costume right here."

Mr Messenger pulled out some red velvet puffy shorts and a black and gold velvet jacket and then he pulled out a REAL STICK-ON BEARD.

At that moment I stopped talking because one thing I have

always wanted is a stick-on beard. I quite like velvet too.

Mr Messenger said William Shakespeare was the main part in the play but there were lots of

other parts too, including fairies, witches and kings from all of William Shakespeare's most famous plays.

After that, Mr Messenger showed us a video of the play so we could get to know all the different characters. When the video finished Mr Messenger said it was time to tell us which parts we would be playing.

My heart went a bit sinky.

I thought, I'd better not be a
market seller.

I thought, I really want to be
William Shakespeare.

I sat up on my heels because
I wanted Mr Messenger to
notice me. Then I sat up a bit
higher because sometimes Mr
Messenger doesn't notice me
even when I am right in front of

him, jumping up and down.

I rubbed my chin with my hands because clever people like William Shakespeare are always doing that.

Mr Messenger looked at his list.

He told Lottie Clark she was Juliet and he told Jordi Bhogal he was Romeo and then he read out lots of other names but I could not remember them all because I was thinking of all the clever things I could do if I was William Shakespeare, e.g joined-up writing.

Mr Messenger looked at me. "Mabel Chase," he said. "You

will be playing..."

I was so excited.

I couldn't wait to try on that beard.

"... Titania!" said Mr Messenger, all chirpety.

I did not smile back.

I did not feel one bit chirpety.

I knew from the video that Titania was NOT a good part.

Titania wears a fairy costume

and falls asleep.

Titania BARELY
EVEN SPEAKS.

Also, Titania
does not have an
interesting beard.

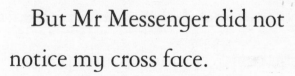

But Mr Messenger did not
notice my cross face.

Mr Messenger was too
busy telling Torin Ray that
HE was going to be William

Shakespeare!

This is why life isn't even fair.

Mr Messenger gave us our costumes and told us to hang them on our pegs in the school hall. Then he told us to spend the rest of the day "getting into character".

At break time, Torin Ray kept shouting, "I'm William Shakespeare, I'm really clever."

I said, "That is not getting into character, Torin Ray, that is boasting."

But Torin Ray said, "You're just jealous."

At that moment, I think I

may have accidentally poked Torin Ray a teeny bit hard in the tummy.

Except Mrs Pollock who is our lunch time supervisor did not believe it was an accident and she had a quiet chat with me in a corner of the playground.

Mrs Pollock told me to stay away from Torin Ray. But I could not stay away from

Torin Ray because for the next
few weeks we kept having
rehearsals and Torin Ray was on
stage the whole entire time.

But Torin Ray did not learn

his lines and Torin Ray did not get into character either. Torin Ray kept MESSING AROUND.

I tried warning Mr Messenger about Torin Ray but Mr Messenger told me not to interfere.

"Mabel," he said, rubbing his eyes. "Just concentrate on YOUR part."

I told Mr Messenger that I

only had one line to learn and
I had already learned it but Mr
Messenger IGNORED ME.

I could tell that Torin Ray was
going to ruin our class play.

I thought, someone around
here needs to take this play
seriously.

In rehearsals, I concentrated
really hard. I learned Torin
Ray's part in a jiffy.

But it was tricky getting into William Shakespeare's character because I did not have the right clothes and I did not have a beard either.

That's when I remembered about the costumes hanging on our pegs.

One lunch break I sneaked into the school hall and I took the velvet coat and shorts out of the bag on Torin Ray's peg and then I took out the stick-on beard.

As soon as I put on that costume I got straight into William Shakespeare's character.

I was SO clever.

I thought, if I keep this costume for the rest of the day I will be able to learn all

my spellings in a jiffy and Mr
Messenger will be SO pleased.

I put my school clothes over
the velvet costume and I pushed
the beard under my collar.
When the bell rang I went back
to class.

I was William Shakespeare for
the whole afternoon.

I got ten out of ten in my
spellings.

I remembered to start my sentences with capital letters.

I did not find maths blurry – not even once.

I was **A BRAINBOX**.

But brainboxes are

sometimes forgetful about
putting things back on pegs
where they belong.

That's why I had to take Torin
Ray's costume home with me.

I was William Shakespeare at
swimming.

I was William Shakespeare at bedtime.

I was still William Shakespeare on the walk to school the next morning. But the shame about

William Shakespeare is that
he DAWDLES.

That's why I did not get into
school in time to put Torin Ray's
costume back on his peg before
lessons.

And that's also why I had to
wear Torin Ray's costume ALL
MORNING.

I was very clever.

I was also quite hot.

But then Mr Messenger ruined everything.

Mr Messenger said it was time to have our dress rehearsal.

He told us to line up and walk over to the school hall.

He told us to go to our pegs to get our costumes.

Except Torin Ray could not find his costume.

Torin Ray and Mr Messenger

looked everywhere for that
costume of his and I helped them
look for it because helping is a
kind and friendly thing to do.

But then Edward Silitoe spotted a bit of red velvet sticking out from under my school jumper.

Edward Silitoe said, "Mabel Chase has stolen Torin Ray's costume."

Everybody stared at me.

Sophie Simpson said, "Will Mabel Chase go to prison?"Mr Messenger did

not answer. He told me to take off Torin Ray's costume and give it back at once. He said he was EXTREMELY DISAPPOINTED.

At this point I was a bit worried because I did not fancy going to prison.

I tried explaining to Mr Messenger about having to borrow the costume because it made me as clever as William Shakespeare and it helped me get ten out of ten in my spelling test but Mr Messenger said, "That's enough, Mabel", so I put on my Titania costume and did not say one more word.

The dress rehearsal did not go well.

Torin Ray could not remember one

single line.

Mr Messenger started to get fidgety.

I did not like to see that teacher of mine getting fidgety.

I thought, it's a good job SOMEONE around here has made the effort to learn William Shakespeare's part.

I marched across the stage to Torin Ray and I told him to

listen carefully.

When Torin Ray forgot his lines, I whispered the right line to him in a CLEAR and CONFIDENT voice.

Then, when I had done ALL

THE HARD WORK, I raced back to the forest to be Titania.

Mr Messenger stopped being fidgety. He rubbed his eyes and he smiled.

He turned to Mrs Woodlea and said, "I think perhaps we might need TWO William Shakespeares for tomorrow's performance."

Mr Messenger asked me if I

thought I could manage to be William Shakespeare as well as Titania.

I looked at Mr Messenger all carefully because I did not want to ruin my chances.

I said, "Playing two parts is not a problem for me but the problem is there is only one William Shakespeare costume and there is only one beard."

I said, "Who will wear it, me or Torin Ray?"

I said, "That is my point."

Mr Messenger sighed and went over to the prop cupboard. He pulled out a red silk cloak. He said, "Perhaps one of you could wear this?"

Torin Ray jumped up, all excited. Torin Ray said, "Ooh, I love that red silk cloak! Can I wear it?!"

I did not even glance at Torin Ray.

I was too busy thinking.

I thought, I bet that red silk cloak has special powers.

I thought, if I wear that red silk cloak I might turn into a superhero.

Suddenly I knew what I had to do.

I had to save the day.

"That is very kind of you, Torin Ray," I said. "But don't worry, I'LL wear the silk one."

I said, "When it comes to costumes I am not fussy."

3

Magnificent Mabel
and the
Dog Show

I'll tell you what's more fun than going on holiday.

Dog shows, that's what.

Lottie Clark goes to dog shows all the time because she has a Labrador puppy OF HER OWN.

Lottie Clark takes dog shows SERIOUSLY.

My family does not take dog shows seriously.

When it comes to dog shows my family is quite cruel.

In my whole life I have not been to one single dog show.

Sometimes I don't know what I have done to deserve that family of mine.

Every August there is a dog show near to where we live but I am not allowed to go to that dog show because my family drags me on holiday to the countryside instead.

Mum and Dad think the countryside is better than dog shows but they have got their facts wrong.

In the countryside we have

to go for long walks.

In the countryside it normally rains.

Whenever I try explaining to my family that I would LOVE to cancel the countryside and go to a dog show instead, they laugh.

They tell me that going

to the countryside is the best
fun ever. They say it is a treat.
But they are wrong because one
thing I'm not keen on is getting
stung by nettles.

I quite like fossil hunting
and I don't MIND paddling in
streams – but fossil hunting and
streams are NOT as good as dog
shows.

This summer I asked Dad if

he would cancel the countryside
so we could go to a dog show
instead.

"Mabel," said Dad. "You can't
go to a dog show without a
dog."

"But I HAVE a dog," I said in
a REALLY POLITE VOICE.

I reminded Dad about
Dermot, who is black and white
and really friendly, especially at

night when it is dark.

Dad said, "I meant a REAL dog, not a toy", and he then ruffled my hair.

This made me quite stompy.

Also, it made me kick the table with the toes of my old brown boots that Mum says still fit me and have to last me until Christmas – even though they are WAY TOO SMALL AND PINCH MY TOES.

Anyway,

Dad has got his facts wrong.

Dog shows are for everyone.

Dog shows are welcoming and FRIENDLY.

That's what Lottie Clark says and when it comes to dog shows Lottie Clark knows more than my dad.

Lottie Clark says if I went to a dog show with Dermot I would have the time of my life and I

believe her because Lottie Clark
is not even a liar.

That is why my heart went
all flippety last Monday when
we were out and about and I
saw a poster for a dog show that
was happening nearby THIS
WEEKEND.

"Dad," I said. "Are we going
on holiday to the countryside
this weekend?"

Dad laughed and said, "Not that I'm aware of."

So I showed him the poster.

"Can we go?" I said, all pleady.

I was getting ready

to make a loud fuss but Dad said, "I don't see why not."

I could not believe it.

I squeezed Dad's hand really hard.

I skipped all the way home.

I was so happy because I could not stop thinking about the dog show.

I thought about the dog

agility competition because Lottie Clark said it is her FAVOURITE.

I thought about the dog fancy dress because Lottie Clark says it is HILARIOUS.

I thought about eating pink candyfloss

with my fingers because Lottie
Clark says they sell pink
candyfloss at the dog show and
it is DELICIOUS.

The day before the dog show I
could not stop practising being
a dog trainer, not even when Mr
Messenger said it was time for a
story.

And even though Lottie Clark
knows A LOT about dogs, my

dog training was a bit more professional than hers.

After school, I went straight up to my bedroom to get Dermot. He was sitting on his patch of floor by the radiator.

Dermot wagged his tail and then Dermot gave a friendly bark.

I had a good long think and then I took Dermot into the garden.

At first Dermot did not want
to learn new tricks but I did not
give up.

I thought, no one said being a
dog trainer was easy.

I thought, I'll just have to
keep trying.

I whistled at Dermot.

I said, "Heel."

I gave him lots of treats. I was

SO patient.

Then, finally, when it was starting to turn dark, Dermot got the message. He jumped through a hoop at top speed. He shook my hand. He did a whole

obstacle course in 6.7 seconds.

He was such a good boy.

I thought, I can't wait to enter Dermot in the dog show tomorrow.

The next morning I ate breakfast at toppity speed because I was so excited.

I packed my red rucksack and I put in my whistle and some treats and then I popped Dermot

in right at the
top with his
nose poking
out so he could
still breathe.

We drove to
the dog show
and luckily Dermot did not
make a sound. He did not even
scrabble. He was SUCH a good
dog.

We parked in a big field and then we walked to a smaller field where the dog show was happening.

Straightaway Lottie Clark ran up to me and she had a blue silk rosette pinned to her top.

She said, "Me and Rollo got second prize in the puppy class!"

Rollo was bouncing around all over the place.

I thought, that puppy could
do with some proper training.

I thought, no wonder Lottie
Clark did not come first.

But I did not say this to Lottie
Clark because I did not want
to break her feelings so I said,
"Well done", and then I followed
her to the main arena.

In the middle of the main
arena was a woman with a

megaphone. She kept shouting,
"Dog agility! Last call for
entries!" in a really bossy voice.

I looked at the dog agility
course. It was not even tricky.

I looked at the three dogs on
leads in the middle of the arena.
They were jumping up and
barking. They did look AT ALL
well trained.

I unzipped my red backpack

and I took Dermot out and then I put Dermot on a lead. I ducked under the railing and I walked Dermot into the middle of the arena.

Dermot did not jump up and he did not bark.

I thought, thank goodness Dermot is SUCH a well-trained dog.

"Hello," said a woman judge.

"And who do we have here?"
I said, "This is Dermot."
The woman chuckled and
winked at another
judge. She

thought I could not notice her
winking but I could because I
am a noticing sort of person.
But I did not get cross or stampy
because I did not want to upset

Dermot.

Me and Dermot watched the three other dogs take turns at the agility course.

The first dog ran out of the arena and barked.

The second dog would not go through the tunnel, not

even when

his owner

sat down at the other end and

offered him a sausage. The third

dog stood on top of the seesaw

and did not come down.

I had never seen such badly

trained dogs.

When it was our turn I said,

"Come on, Dermot" and we set off through the agility course.

It wasn't even TRICKY.

But after a while I heard lots of loud barking and when I looked behind I got a BIG shock. Behind us were those three

naughty dogs and they were
chasing Dermot.

Me and Dermot ran a bit
faster but the dogs just followed
us into the tunnel and out again.

We sprinted up over the
seesaw but those naughty dogs

followed us over that too.

We jumped for our lives through the hoops but they just jumped after us.

Then when we crossed the finish line they caught up with us and the biggest dog picked Dermot up and licked him LIKE HE WAS A TOY.

The crowd clapped and cheered and LAUGHED.

I WAS SO CROSS.

I thought, Lottie Clark was wrong. This dog show is not kind and welcoming. This dog show is quite dangerous.

I found an old biscuit in my pocket and I held it out for that naughty dog.

I said, "Drop" in a really firm voice.

Then I said, "Or else" in an

even firmer voice.

Luckily that naughty dog dropped Dermot and gobbled up the biscuit.

Then I picked Dermot up and stomped out of the arena. But at that moment there was an announcement on the loud speaker.

"Ladies and gentlemen!" said a crackly voice. "The winner of this year's dog agility not only managed a clear round in record time, he also managed to show the other dogs how to do it too. This year's winner of the dog agility is ... Dermot!"

The crowd clapped and cheered and whistled and someone shouted, "Go, Dermot!" in a really loud voice.

The judge walked over to me

and Dermot and handed me a silk rosette. It was bright red and it said "Champion" in shiny gold writing.

I pinned the rosette on to Dermot's collar and I said thank you to the rude judge because that is called being polite and then I went to show the rosette to Mum and Dad and Meg.

Dad looked at Dermot and

smiled.

"You were right, Mabel," he said. "You don't need a real dog to go to a dog show."

Mum and Meg smiled too.

But I did not smile.

I thought, how rude.

I thought, I don't know why they keep saying Dermot isn't a real dog.

I thought, Dermot is a

champion.

Then I put my arms around Dermot and I hugged him tightly all the way home.